The Ultimate Teacher Gift

by
Cailey Appenzeller

ISBN-13: 978-1-946617-99-6
ISBN-10: 1-946617-99-7

TABLE OF CONTENTS

Chapter 1 _____ 1

Chapter 2 _____ 5

Chapter 3 _____ 11

Chapter 4 _____ 19

Chapter 5 _____ 25

Chapter 6 _____ 33

Chapter 7 _____ 41

Chapter 8 _____ 45

Chapter 9 _____ 55

Chapter 10 _____ 61

Chapter 11 _____ 65

Chapter 12 _____ 71

Chapter 13 _____ 79

Chapter 14 _____ 83

Chapter 15 _____ 105

About the Book _____ 109

This book is dedicated to Mr. Pontius, who taught me that my weaknesses are simply strengths in hiding.

I'll miss his thumbs up and hearty laugh in class. No matter what, Mr. Pontius will always be my teacher.

I'd like to thank my mom,
who edited and co-wrote this story.
She helped shape and craft
my idea into a chapter book.

Thanks for helping me
turn a dream into a reality.

The Ultimate Teacher Gift

Chapter 1

I'm leaving

I held a sheet of paper filled with words from my teacher, but those were the only two I saw. They weren't a surprise, but they were a shock, like when you stick your finger in an electric socket. Not that I'd tried it.

Staring at the words, I slid a chair away from the kitchen table and sat. The sizzle of ground beef my mom was stirring faded into the background. It's taco aroma no longer held appeal.

Five weeks ago, Mr. P had asked our class for volunteers to speak with a group of adults who were interviewing him for a principal position at another middle school. I'd volunteered to be part of it. Why not? Mr. P was easy to talk about, even for me. He was the reason I could speak in any group setting at all.

The letter he'd sent home today confirmed my expectation: he'd gotten the job. It was a great opportunity for him. He could influence more students as a principal than as a teacher, and I was living proof he worked miracles.

Mr. P had been my humanities teacher for two years at Addison-Dewey Lower Middle School. I wouldn't have him again even if he stayed, but I still got a hole in my gut every time I thought about him not being around. Today's letter made it worse. The countdown had officially started, and now our time with Mr. P was quickly dwindling.

"Is something wrong?" Mom nodded toward the paper in my hands as she placed a stack of dinner plates on the table.

My younger brother Brody peeked over my shoulder. "Mouse got the note."

"Stop calling your sister that. She has a perfectly good name. Right, Cassie?" Mom pushed the plates toward my brother and motioned for him to set the table.

"Everyone calls her that." Rolling his eyes, he distributed six plates around the kitchen table in a haphazard array. "It's the note about Mr. P leaving. Everyone's posting about it." He turned to leave, but mom's finger told him to stay. He released a dramatic sigh. "I don't know why Mouse is so upset. I'm the one who doesn't have a chance of getting him as a teacher now."

"I'm not upset." That wasn't the right word, but I didn't have anything more accurate. Billions of words in the English language and none that fit. "It's just…a big change." A brilliant explanation. Mr. P would be so proud.

Mom returned from the island with a handful of silverware that she placed on the table in the middle of the plate minefield. Then tapping my shoulder, she pointed to the letter. "May I read it?"

Staring at the sheet wouldn't change the words, and I wasn't sure I wanted that anyway. I gave her the paper.

While Mom read, Brody randomly distributed silverware then escaped before she finished. When she lifted her head, her eyebrows were furrowed. "What do you think about this?"

"I don't know." It was the truth, and it was frustrating. Mr. P often praised my insight and depth. So far all I had was: *It's a big change.*

Mom patted my knee and returned the paper. "Mr. P will make a fantastic principal."

"I know." It was the only thing I was sure about.

Chapter 2

The next day, the school was buzzing like a hive full of hyper bees. Kids zipped through the hallways asking if others had heard about Mr. P's announcement. Theories about why he was leaving emerged: a dare, a lost bet, the witness protection program, and my personal favorite: his superhero identity had been compromised.

After closing my locker, I carried my binder to algebra, my first class of the day. It wouldn't start for another twenty minutes, but I entered the classroom to find my friends.

Pictures of Einstein with nerdy inspirational quotes decorated the walls, and rows of tables covered the tile floors. Though Mrs. Garcia kept her room neat, the air smelled like marker. The cheap kind.

Three of my friends sat in chairs around a table

in the middle of the classroom, snacking on the remains of breakfast. When I joined them, they stopped talking and turned their attention to me.

"What do you think about Mr. P's news?" Liz pushed her glasses higher on her nose and then brushed a stray hair away from her face as if clearing the way for a brilliant response.

Wished I had one. Better to keep the attention on their opinions. "I don't know. What do you think?"

"We should get him a gift." Phoebe bit into her apple, then said, "That's what my dad's firm does when employees retire." Apple bits sprayed onto the desk.

Grimacing, Zeke brushed the pieces onto the floor then he wiped his palms on his pants. "Mr. P isn't retiring,"

"He's retiring from teaching." With an eyebrow raised in a challenge, Liz opened her bag of granola.

"He'll never retire from teaching." Zeke shook apple bits off his sneaker. "It's who he is."

"Okay. He's retiring from the official employment position of teacher." Liz tilted her head, punctuating her point. Her glasses travelled down her nose like a kid on a sliding board, but she pushed them back into place before they fell off.

"And for what it's worth, I think a gift is a great idea."

It was, but not just any gift. "We need to get him something special."

"Better than special." Phoebe's eyes gleamed with intensity, and she chomped her apple. "It has to be perfect."

"Agreed." Zeke kicked apple bits across the tiled floor, clearing a spot around him. "But what would make the perfect gift?"

"Cookies." Leo and his loud mouth wandered to our table. His partner in crime, Tyler the tower, and a few other boys joined too.

Leo swiped Phoebe's apple and bit it. When he offered to return it, Phoebe scowled and shook her head. Her fingers curled into fists, but she sat on them. Last week, Mr. P had challenged her to be more collaborative. Leo would test her resolve.

He said, "My mom could make a couple dozen, maybe a variety of cookies. Mr. P would probably share with us, right?"

"It's not about you." Phoebe zipped her binder closed, concealing a bag of carrots inside.

"Should be." He took another bite of the apple while his gaze roamed our table, probably looking for other food to *share*.

"You have problems." Liz frowned at Leo and pocketed her bag of granola. She surveyed the crowd growing around our table. "Any other ideas?"

"Steak, potatoes, and corn, with chocolate cake for dessert."

When Tyler spoke, I tilted my face up to check his expression. He had to be joking.

He shrugged. "Guys like food."

An argument erupted, guys in agreement, girls protesting.

Accident Ava stumbled into the mess, her curls bouncing as she bumped into one student then the next. The crowd cleared a path, and she managed to make it to our table without knocking anyone over. "Maybe we could make a card and write messages inside. That would be a personal gift, and if it was from the whole class, that would make it special."

That would make it a miracle. I bit my tongue.

"A card's too much work." Leo's face contorted as if in pain, and his cohorts grimaced in agreement. He continued, "And what if we used bad grammar or spelling? After all his effort to teach us…" He shook his head. "I, for one, think that would be a disappointing gift."

"You could use a grammar and spell checker." Zeke turned from Leo and lifted his chin toward me. "Any ideas, Mouse? You're the creative one."

Why hadn't I thought about this? I shook my head.

Phoebe snapped her fingers. "Gift certificate." She nodded as if agreeing with herself. Maybe she was convincing herself. "When the people at my dad's firm don't know what to give someone, they contribute to a gift certificate. Maybe we could get one for a nice restaurant."

"I'll go with him." Leo rubbed his stomach. "It's depressing to eat by yourself."

"You don't seem to have a problem with it." Tyler slapped the back of his friend's head. "Besides, he'd take his wife."

"Don't mess the hair." Leo shoved Tyler, and a wrestling match broke out.

Five guys joined. Bodies tangled as they rolled on the ground, alternating between tackling and teasing each other. Best friends. Guys were weird.

Mrs. Garcia entered the room. Her heels clicked as she made her way to the tangled throng of boys rolling in apple bits. "Gentlemen. You have ten seconds to get into your chairs before you stay after school solving math problems with me."

In less than five seconds, they'd found their seats.

Zeke, who'd stayed out of the mess, tapped my elbow and whispered, "Whatever you come up with, I want in. You'll figure out the ultimate teacher gift." He turned in his seat and faced the smart board.

I stared at the back of his head. He had more confidence than I did. We needed a special gift, and the clock was ticking.

Chapter 3

"Does anyone have questions about the letter you received last night?" Mr. P pulled up a chair in front of a white board covered with Calvin and Hobbes comic strips, and sat. Slouching, he put his hands behind his head then waited.

All day long our class had argued over gift ideas as we moved from one classroom to the next. No one had discussed anything other than the *perfect* gift, so now, during the last class of the day, we had no questions to ask Mr. P about his departure, despite his willingness to discuss it.

Students glanced at each other as if expecting someone to speak up. Thankfully, no one looked at me. The questions I had weren't ones I'd ask in front of an audience. Would he miss teaching? Would he miss us?

Leo raised his hand and blurted, "What would

be a perfect going away gift?"

So much for it being a surprise.

Tyler raised his long arm as if to slap the back of Leo's head again, but put it down. One threat of afternoon detention must be enough for the day.

Mr. P chuckled, sat up in his chair, and put his hands on his knees. "No gifts are necessary, but if you, or your parents, are determined to ignore that, I could make a list to give you some ideas."

"Yes." Grinning, Leo scanned the room as if expecting accolades.

Instead, students shook their heads. Some covered their faces with their hands. Tyler mouthed, "You idiot."

"What?" Leo shrugged. "Just clarifying. It's what leaders do." He turned to Mr. P. "You taught us that, right?"

Mr. P scratched his head and mumbled, "So much to do. So little time."

Was he quoting from a book? Mr. P's room was lined with shelves of paperbacks ranging from historical nonfiction to dystopian YA. One of his favorite pastimes was to match students to stories and make recommendations. Generally, the fit was either perfect for our tastes, or a challenge for our growth.

Mr. P loved growth mindsets.

"Could we throw you a party?" Ava's eyebrows rose. She almost fell out of her seat as she turned to glance at Phoebe and Liz, who nodded their approval.

Mr. P scratched his chin in an evil villain manor, but then his expression brightened. "That's a great idea! Why don't you organize it, and we'll see when we can fit it on the calendar. We've got a lot of year-end activities that we'll have to work around."

As the class erupted with suggestions, Zeke turned in his chair to face me. "A party isn't the perfect gift, and you know Mr. P will come up with a gift list that's for other people. Have you figured something out yet?"

Why did he keep asking me? Anyone could come up with a great idea, and hopefully someone would soon. I shook my head.

"Let me know when you do." He turned around in his seat and slouched, waiting out our classmates who continued to barrage Mr. P with party suggestions.

Within minutes, our teacher morphed party planning into a free write assignment on our hopes for the summer. As if to prove a point, clouds parted and the sun beamed into our classroom.

Over the following hour, the temperature inside steadily rose along with the odor of more than one boy who'd forgotten to use deodorant this morning. While we baked, noise faded, except for the sound of keyboards clicking and the occasional slurp of a water bottle.

During the last five minutes of class, students stared at the clock as if willing it to speed up. I wanted it to slow down, but at the moment, I was more concerned about my shorts.

Thanks to the oven our room had become, my butt was sticking to the plastic chair. I'd seen and heard others get out of sweaty seats, and it wasn't something I wanted to mimic in front of an audience. I'd have to wait for the rest to leave before I extracted myself.

Static noise came from the intercom.

"Please get ready for afternoon announcements." A voice, sounding much like a salesman's, echoed through the room. As it droned on, I mouthed the words in sync with the speaker. After three years of listening to the same scripted closing, the words had etched into my brain.

My classmates returned their computers to the storage unit and plugged them into the outlets to repower for tomorrow. Conversations overshadowed the announcements, but Mr. P allowed it. Apparently, he wasn't interested in hearing them either.

"Students may be dismissed at their teacher's discretion."

No sooner had the announcer's words filtered through the classroom conversation, than students grabbed their binders and left.

When the last person exited, I shut down my computer and closed it.

"Cassie."

Mr. P hadn't left with my classmates. I straightened in my seat, careful not to move my butt a centimeter.

He sat in a chair across from me and propped his legs on the table between us. "I talked with Bill Smith. He was on the search committee that interviewed you and other kids about me as a principal candidate. Bill was impressed with all of you."

Was he impressed by what we'd said or how we'd said it? I wasn't about to ask and extend the conversation. My muscles ached for motion, but I remained glued to my seat.

Mr. P shifted his glasses from his nose to the top of his head. "He mentioned one student shared with surprising depth. Said she had dark brown hair in a ponytail, and deep brown eyes that pierced your soul."

He probably added that last one for effect.

"Bill didn't know her name because she took her nametag off." He arched an eyebrow at me. "Of course, I knew he was referring to you."

My face heated, taking with it my body temperature, which didn't help my chair situation. "The name tag wasn't sticking."

Laughing, he pushed up his sagging sleeves. "I just wanted to encourage you with that."

Awkward silence. Was I supposed to respond or wait?

"You're growing for sure." He gave me a double thumbs up. "Taking bigger chances, leading without people realizing it, working on that growth mindset."

Of course, *growth mindset* was going to make its way into the conversation at some point.

I smiled.

He nodded.

Awkward silence again.

As much as I loved talking with Mr. P, the ending was often confusing. I never knew when or how to close out our conversations. But I'd learned enough to guess he was probably waiting for me to lead. "Thank you."

"Of course."

Were we done? I thought so, but I didn't dare move from my seat.

We stared at each other for another moment.

He tapped the table with his fingers then stood. When I didn't move, he jerked his thumb toward the door. "I have to meet up with someone. Have a good afternoon."

He left the room, and I whispered a prayer of thanks, then set about unsticking my butt from the chair.

Chapter 4

The next morning at school, I dodged kids milling around my algebra table and took my seat.

"Mom's willing to make cookies." Leo tossed a piece of popcorn in the air and caught it in his mouth. He coughed and hacked, then swallowed. "Just sayin'."

"Just choking." Tyler smacked his friend on the back, twice, three times, before Leo shoved him away.

Liz put her arm between the two boys, preventing another rumble. "Cookies aren't personal enough." When the boys remained in place, she lowered her arm. "We need something more relational, more significant."

"Exactly." Ava excitedly waved her hands in the air as if conjuring a spell, a sure sign someone was about to get smacked in the face. "We should make him a card and write personal notes."

"Guys don't do that." Leo shoved a handful of popcorn in his mouth. Crumbs fell on Phoebe's binder, and he mumbled, "It's too girly."

"Then the guys can give him their own gift." Glaring, Phoebe dusted crumbs off her binder and onto Leo's sneakers.

"Maybe we will." Crossing his arms, Leo nodded at Tyler who looked less confident about that idea.

A card? Cookies? Those were the best ideas we could come up with? Twenty-four hours had passed since the gift idea sprouted, yet none of us had anything special enough for Mr. P.

I'd wracked my brain all night, but my imagination had been dominated by images of Ava cutting her tongue on an envelope and Leo eating Mr. P's gift.

On cue, Ava extracted a pencil from her binder and broke it in the process. Liz handed her another one. As if not to be outdone, Phoebe ripped blank pages from her notebook and offered them too. Ava began drafting a card, and a group of girls surrounded her.

Leo huffed and feasted on popcorn until a

rubber band hit his nose. Tyler and a few guys laughed and launched more at him.

While rubber bands sailed through the air, a thought nagged at my mind, something Zeke had said yesterday, "You'll figure out the ultimate teacher gift."

Maybe it was an impossible task. Mr. P wasn't just any teacher. He knew each of his students—their strengths and weaknesses—and knew how to challenge and encourage them to be their best.

Regardless of the skill-level or attitude, he made a difference in *all* his students' lives, not just the ones he liked. And no one knew who he liked or didn't because he invested in all of us. Humanities came alive in his presence because the classroom wasn't just about reading books and writing reports.

Like a meteorite crashing onto Mar's surface, an idea hit me. Mr. P was a humanities teacher. He loved *stories*.

My heart pounded, and I raised my voice to be heard above the chatter. "We should write a book."

The girls stopped working on the card, and the boys paused their rubber band war. Liz's eyebrows arched, mirroring the confused expressions on the others' faces. "A...book?"

Was it an odd suggestion? He was a humanities teacher. It seemed so perfect.

The others didn't appear as excited.

I swallowed the lump growing in my throat. "We can call it *The Ultimate Teacher Gift*."

Around the table, guys and girls exchanged less-than-enthusiastic glances. Maybe they didn't understand the vision.

"It's personal." I gestured to the girls. "And you can have fun with it." I turned to the boys.

The two groups stared at me, and silence hung over the table. After what seemed like an eternity, Leo broke it. "That'll take forever."

The guys murmured in agreement, "Too much work," as if that were a legitimate excuse. Time might be an issue, but effort was not. This was Mr. P.

As I opened my mouth to lobby for my idea, a rubber band smacked the side of Tyler's face, and the war restarted, all thought of a book left behind.

The girls avoided eye contact with me and returned to working on their card. Even Phoebe joined in, maybe to offer support to Ava, but more likely because of the collaboration challenge Mr. P had extended to her.

Whatever the reason, I was on my own. And

maybe it was better this way. Artistic freedom.

Between the chatter and flying objects, it was impossible to concentrate, so I relocated to a remote part of the classroom, a corner decorated with geometric shapes and equations. There I retrieved a pencil from my binder and held it like a warrior wielding a valiant weapon. My focus muted the distractions around me almost as well as a set of earplugs would have.

Mr. P's words echoed in my mind. "The easiest thing to write about is what inspires you."

What inspired me? Friends. Creativity. Mr. P.

I tapped the rounded pencil tip against my notebook, leaving gray dots on the white page. After a few seconds, a cloud-like image emerged. It reminded me someone once said, "A picture is worth a thousand words."

That was as good a place as any to start.

Chapter 5

As the school day wore on, a storm moved in. Rain pelted the windows of Mr. P's classroom. No fear of being trapped by the chair of stickiness today.

Though the time until the school year's end was counting down too quickly, the clock in Mr. P's room worked in my favor. Unlike many of my classmates, I finished my free write early, which meant freedom to do whatever I wanted.

I pulled a blank piece of lined paper out of my binder, and my cover sketch came with it. Mr. P couldn't see that. Not until the book was done. I grabbed the picture, intent on getting it back into my binder ASAP.

"Is that the book cover?" Zeke whispered across the table. He pointed to the drawing in my hand.

If he made fun of it, I'd never work on this at school again.

I nodded.

"It's great." He reached for it, but his hand stopped above the paper. His eyebrows arched in request. When I nodded, he tugged the picture closer. "I knew you'd come up with something amazing. Can I join?"

It was the first positive feedback I'd received, but I couldn't take any chances. "It has to stay a secret."

"Of course." He returned the sketch to me. While he glanced over his shoulder at Mr. P, who was typing on his computer, I tucked the sketch back into my binder. Then I returned to the lined sheet waiting on the table for me, and unsheathed my pencil sword.

Zeke dragged his chair to my side of the table. "What's our excuse if he asks what we're doing?"

"What do you suggest?"

Scratching his head, he scanned the room. His gaze landed on a calendar, and he smiled. "Mother's Day gift. If he asks, I'll do the talking. Part of my contribution to the gift."

An excellent contribution. "Be my guest."

"Okay. So, what else can I do?"

The cover concept was sketched out, but the actual story was still missing. I bent over the blank sheet, my pencil poised to write. "Just hand me ideas."

"Ideas?" Ava turned a full 180 in the chair behind me and slid off the seat. Using the back of my chair for leverage, she pulled herself up. "I'm great at those. If you need ideas for your story, I can help."

"You're working on a card." Zeke sat straighter and stuck out his chest. "And Mouse already has an idea specialist." Twisting, he leaned closer to me forcing Ava to back up.

She almost fell again, but steadied herself using my hair. Her fingers had caught my ponytail and yanked strands tight like a medieval torture rack. Tears came to my eyes. "Could you let go, please?"

"Oh, sorry about that." Ava untangled herself. "Anyway, we gave up on the card. Couldn't agree on what it should look like, and without everyone writing a message, it didn't seem that special..." Her gaze shifted to my binder, where a corner of my sketch peeked out.

She snatched the paper. I lunged for it, but stopped. Knowing Ava, she'd accidentally rip it if I tried to get it back. Her mouth dropped open. "This is cool. Did you think of maybe writing a romance?"

The design—sunlight slicing through dark clouds to reveal the title—didn't remotely hint at a romance, which I'd never write anyway.

"Did someone say romance?" Phoebe turned and scooted her chair into the spot where Zeke's had been. "Who is it this time?" Her eyes surveyed the other students.

"It's not people in class." Zeke glanced at our teacher, who was still working on his computer. He whispered, "It's the book we're writing for Mr. P."

"Mouse is writing a romance story for Mr. P?" Liz joined the party, sliding her chair next to Phoebe's. Disbelief covered Liz's face, and she glanced at my blank paper. "Haven't gotten too far, have you?"

"We're just throwing out ideas." Zeke rubbed his temples as if chasing away a headache. Or maybe he was trying telekinesis to remove the others.

It wouldn't work. I'd tried that myself. Many times.

"A romance would be brilliant, right?" Ava grinned like she thought herself a genius. She dropped my sketch on the table.

Phoebe and Liz reached for it, but I snagged the paper before they could touch it. "This has to stay a secret." I returned the drawing to my binder, this time securing it inside.

"What if the protagonist was a lost orphan?" Ava bounced on her toes, her curls moving like springs, her mouth picking up speed. "And once she finds her true love, they become runaways!" She squealed and stepped back, bumping the table behind her. A water bottle teetered on its edge then crashed onto the floor.

Mr. P cleared his throat. He put his finger to his lips.

Message received by all, except the one it was intended for.

Ava returned to our table. "What do you think?"

"Oh, that's not cliché at all," Phoebe said.

Liz snorted then coughed, but at least she hadn't ganged up against our friend.

We didn't need relational tension. We needed a common project. "Romance isn't my genre, but you could write a story for him. And maybe Phoebe and Liz could help you while Zeke and I work on a different story. The more, the better."

The girls stopped snickering. Liz blinked. Phoebe's eyes narrowed at me, and then she smiled at Ava. "Sure. We can work out the kinks later. And maybe Mouse could draw a bat for our cover."

Lines appeared on Ava's forehead. "Why a bat?"

"Because," Phoebe said and smirked, "there's obviously going to be a vampire involved."

Ava's forehead wrinkles disappeared. "Vampire love!"

"Runaway vampire love!" Phoebe elbowed Liz, who finally stopped blinking. "With a Mouse-designed romance cover."

Liz shook her head. "I don't know about—"

"That's alright, cause I do." Ava clapped by my ear, sending a wave of volume and pressure into my head.

Wincing, I pushed a blank sheet of paper to Phoebe. "I'm not sure when I'll get to the cover, or what it'll look like. Remember romance isn't my genre."

"Of course." Ava nodded as if I suffered from some sort of fatal disease that she'd just have to work around. Then she pointed at Liz and Phoebe and motioned for them to follow her. "We should brainstorm more ideas."

Phoebe yanked Liz out of her seat and dragged her toward Ava. When they reached the far end of the table, they sat.

Liz rested her head in her hands, her eyes closed, while Ava and Phoebe crouched over the lined piece of paper. Phoebe barked orders, and Ava furiously wrote. Maybe Phoebe was invested. Maybe she was on a collaboration mission. Either way, she'd embraced my hint to not damage the friendship. Hopefully Liz would too.

Their departure left Zeke and me with a blank piece of paper and a quiet space. No excuses for not making progress.

"You know, I prefer it this way." Zeke tilted his head toward the far end of the table. "Mom always said, 'Too many cooks ruin the soup.'"

I hoped that wasn't true of books too.

Chapter 6

Another day, another algebra class.

"Did you see Mr. P's gift list?" Liz cleaned her glasses with her shirt and returned them to her face.

Glancing around the room, Phoebe sneaked a carrot out of her binder and popped it into her mouth. "Donations to the Discretionary Student Support Fund. A list of books to leave for the teacher who will replace him." Bits of carrots dribbled out of her mouth onto the table. She dusted them off. "Everything on the list was for someone else."

"As expected." Zeke kicked carrot bits off his sneakers. "That's why we need to get him something special. Did you come up with anything yet, Mouse?"

"I thought you two were working together?" Ava pulled out a small stack of papers and grabbed her pen.

"We are, but we had some artistic differences and needed a break to recalibrate." He turned to me. "This was your project from the start. I'm just helping, so we should go the direction you prefer."

I hated him giving up his idea, but when we'd tried to merge concepts during Mr. P's class, it hadn't gone well, and we'd lost a lot of time. My thoughts had jumbled with his competing thoughts, and I hadn't been able to write any words on the blank sheet.

Zeke preferred an epic fantasy with ogres and dwarfs. I'd been thinking action adventure with spies or ninjas. The more he and I had talked, the more tangled my thoughts had become. So I'd asked if we could revisit it tomorrow, which was today.

My gut tightened. "Are you sure you're okay with giving up your idea?"

"Yes, I promise. Now tell me what we're writing about, spies or ninjas?"

"Actually…" My stomach relaxed, but my heart rate picked up. "I'm planning a science fiction story with a Light Spectrum Master, his apprentice students, and an evil Dark Lord." I removed a new book cover sketch from my binder and slid it across the table to him, drawing side down.

Zeke flipped the sheet and studied it. Smiling, he returned the paper to me, and I secured it inside my binder before the others could peek.

His head bobbed as if warming up to the concept. "Given the genre and characters, I'm sure we can develop a solid story Mr. P will enjoy."

Leo stopped by our table. "He'd never tell you if he didn't like it, but he'll love it just the same."

That made no sense. I glanced at Zeke, and he shook his head.

Leo bit into a giant sourdough pretzel, showering Phoebe's binder in crumbs. A few landed in her hair.

Glaring, she growled and shoved her chair away from the table. Her fingers fisted, but she marched to the trashcan in the corner of the classroom where she bent over the container and raked her fingers through her hair.

"No, I'm serious." Leo took another bite, leaving more pieces for Phoebe to clean when she returned. "Mr. P will love a book, if you can get it done in time."

That could be a problem. We still had to write the story, then edit, and then get it printed so it wasn't just a stack of papers. For this to be a special gift, both content and appearance would be important. I was running out of time.

Leo bit into his pretzel again, and crumbs danced on our tabletop. The crunching sound that emanated from his mouth was deafening.

"Can you please chew with your mouth closed?" Ava clamped her hands over her ears. The pen in her hand left a blue streak along her jaw. "We're trying to make real progress here."

"Who says eating pretzels isn't making progress?" Leo turned to Tyler, who shrugged in response.

Phoebe returned and pushed Leo away from her spot. Then she wiped her arm over the table, herding his crumbs onto the floor. It was one thing to clean her own mess, but a completely different thing to clean Leo's. He should be thankful his arms were still attached.

Instead, he burped and nodded toward the papers in front of Ava. "Are you working on the storybook thing, too?" He took another bite, and crumbs fell onto the floor this time.

Ava pointed to Phoebe and Liz and said, "We're writing our own story, a romance, but we can't agree on our vampire's name. I was about to ask Mouse her opinion, Juan or Hercules?"

"Both sound stupid." Leo lifted his pretzel to bite it, but Tyler grabbed his wrist stopping his progress. Tyler tilted his head toward the girls. Leo's eyebrows rose in confusion.

A character like Leo would make a great apprentice, one who was completely oblivious to those surrounding him. Hmm...

Leo scowled at Tyler then waved his pretzel at Ava. "I vote for Henry."

"You mean Hercules?"

"That's the one." He yanked himself free from Tyler and bit the pretzel again. "Good leaders know how to make decisions."

Liz pushed her binder aside and sat up in her seat, a picture of intelligence and dignity. "We posted an online survey yesterday, asking for the most handsome boys' names. Those were the top two responses. Trust us. We know what we're talking about, and we'll make a *great* decision."

Liz hadn't wanted to work on the project, yet now she was defending it. I stifled a laugh. History proved you didn't want to mess with her. She was stubborn and defensive, and if you started an argument against her, you'd better be prepared to lose.

If Liz and Leo argued, that would dominate conversation, and I wouldn't have to choose the romantic lead's name. I'd dodged a bullet on that one.

"Plus, Mouse is going to make our book cover. Another *great* decision." Ava crossed her arms and nodded to me. "Right?"

There was only so much time between now and the end of the school year. If I was going to finish my book, I wasn't sure how much time I could devote to another one. "Actually..."

Ava said, "But I thought—?"

"Ha!" Leo flipped the pretzel in the air and caught it. "Even Mouse thinks it's stupid."

Tyler slapped the back of Leo's head, and the pretzel flew out of his hand. When Leo spun angrily toward his friend, Ava stood, knocking Leo over, then stumbled to where I sat.

"It is not stupid." She sounded horrified. "Mouse, do you think our book is stupid?"

I froze like a deer in headlights. How had I stumbled into the center of this potentially explosive conversation? As I shook my head, Leo interrupted again.

"Course she does."

"Calm down." Zeke waved his hand in Ava's face, but her gaze remained on me, so he raised his voice. "Mouse never said that. Your issue is with Leo."

Ava turned and locked onto Leo.

Tyler had wrapped his arms around his friend and was dragging him backward. "Dude, what's the matter with you this morning?"

"I'm just leading." He tried to break free. "They'll never have a special gift in time without my help."

"You're not helping." Tyler grabbed for the edge of the table to steady himself, but his hand landed on the back of Liz's chair.

The seat, with Liz still in it, slid back and tilted. Phoebe dove across the table to grab her friend's flailing hands. When they connected, Phoebe's body dragged across the table. In the same moment, Ava marched toward Leo, but her sneaker caught a chair leg, and she stumbled.

Five bodies crashed onto the floor in a heap.

Mrs. Garcia's heels clicked against the tile faster than a machine gun. She hovered over the writhing mess on the floor and pointed to the door. "All of you, to the principal's office. Now."

As our friends untangled, she turned to Zeke and me. "You too."

Chapter 7

Mr. Cone's office wasn't big enough for seven students at one time, but we were crammed in it anyway. We stood in a crooked line in front of our principal's desk. Behind it, he sat in his oversized office chair and rubbed his temples, eyes closed. Light from the window reflected off his bald head making it a challenge to look at him for too long.

"So let me get this straight." He lowered his hands and made eye contact with each of us. "There's been a *misunderstanding* over a farewell gift?"

"Yes, sir."

I cringed at Leo's voice. Why hadn't someone else answered? Why hadn't I answered? Detention, here we come.

"If I may, sir?" Leo stood at attention next to me, staring straight ahead as if in the military.

Where had that come from?

"This should be good." Our principal reached into his desk drawer and removed a bottle of aspirin. "Go ahead, Leo."

"We've been working on a secret project for Mr. P. He's a great teacher, and we wanted to give him something special as a going away present, but there were artistic differences. We're sorry it upset Mrs. Garcia, and we'll be careful to avoid confusion in the future."

"Artistic differences. Confusion." Mr. Cone popped two aspirin in his mouth and swallowed.

"Well, you always encourage us to do our best…"

Was he going to blame this on Mr. Cone?

"…and we've invested our hearts into this project. So when there was a difference of opinion, it had to be worked out."

"With a fight." Mr. Cone returned to rubbing his temples.

"There wasn't a fight, sir." Leo glanced left and right, and the rest of us nodded in agreement. "It was an accident."

Our principal lowered his hands and laughed. "How does an accident leave five students in a heap on the floor?"

"Well..." Ava stepped forward, but she tripped on Tyler's giant sneaker.

He tried to stop her fall, but she stumbled sideways and knocked over Phoebe, who took out Liz. Tyler bumped Mr. Cone's desk, dumping his coffee mug over the side. Brown liquid spread across his gray carpet.

Mr. Cone's mouth opened, and Leo said, "Pretty much like that."

While our friends picked themselves off the floor, Mr. Cone took two more aspirin and retrieved his coffee mug from the carpet. "In light of this... this...information..." He waved his hands at us as if trying to make us disappear. "I want you to see a school counselor if you have any more *artistic differences*. Under no circumstances whatsoever should this particular group of students attempt to work out any problems yourselves. Am I clear?"

Those directions were completely opposite what Mr. P said we should do, but we nodded anyway.

"Sir?" Leo raised his hand then said, "Can you please keep this incident a secret? We don't want Mr. P to know about the gift."

"Of course, I'd never—"

"And can you please order Mrs. Garcia not to mention it to anyone either?"

At Leo's interruption, Mr. Cone's face reddened. "You may respectfully and politely ask her that yourselves." He pointed at the door. "Now, go back to your class—quietly and, above all else, carefully —before I change my mind and give you all detention."

As we exited the office with the silent walk of the guilty, I glanced at the clock. Another hour gone, and still nothing written.

Chapter 8

"Why are you sitting by yourself?" Zeke plopped in the seat next to me and slid his lunch bag onto the table.

Around us, chaos reigned in the form of unleashed energy. Loud chatter and kids popping in and out of seats mixed with an assortment of odors that I tried to ignore. All assaulted my senses. The cafeteria was the worst place to work on anything, let alone something as significant as Mr. P's story, but I had to have it done by the end of next week, and so far, I had nothing.

"We're running out of time, and I don't even have a first line." I shoved my unopened lunch bag to the side so I could write. A blank page stared back at me.

"Maybe you should use the laptop. It's what you're used to writing on." He pulled a sandwich out of his bag and unwrapped it.

The peanut aroma made my mouth water, and I glanced at my own bag. Maybe just a bite. I grabbed a granola bar. "Mr. P can see the files on the laptop." Sweet honey and chocolate melted on my tongue. The oats would fill my gurgling stomach, and the fuel might help me think. "Pencil and paper aren't the problem. I just can't figure out how to begin."

After swallowing, Zeke said, "Start with the obvious."

There was nothing obvious about writing an opening hook. Hadn't he heard anything Mr. P had been teaching us? "Do you have a suggestion?"

"A long time ago, in a galaxy far, far away..." He laughed. "You know. The start of every movie in that famous franchise-which-shall-not-be-named."

"You want to copy someone else's line? That's not original. I'm not even sure it's legal."

"Imitation is the highest form of praise." He shrugged. "Mr. P said that once."

Maybe it wasn't a terrible idea, but it didn't seem creative enough.

"Why are we sitting at this table today?" Liz slid onto the seat next to me, and Phoebe sat on her other side.

So much for finding a place to myself.

"Mouse needed a change of location to spark her creativity. How's *your* book going?" Zeke took another bite of his sandwich.

Phoebe and Liz exchanged a glance then Liz said, "Ava pulled the plug on it. The visit to Mr. Cone's office freaked her out. She's in the counseling office crying."

"We wanted to help her, but Ava said she needed time alone to regroup." Phoebe pulled out an apple. "Hard to imagine one visit to Cone's office could do that to a person."

"I tried to make it easy on you guys." Leo placed his tray on the table next to Phoebe, and Tyler sat next to him.

Both had chosen macaroni and cheese, mashed potatoes, applesauce and chocolate pudding. Their trays were oozing gelatinous substances.

I used my granola bar like smelling salts to keep my stomach from revolting.

"Why are you sitting with us?" Phoebe moved her apple into her other hand, the one away from Leo.

"This is where we always sit." Tyler shoveled macaroni and cheese into his mouth and swallowed without chewing. "We thought you were joining us."

How had I not paid attention to where I'd chosen to sit? I grabbed my bag and stood. "Sorry. I didn't realize I stole your spot."

Tyler raised his hand. "We don't mind. The rest of the guys can find another place to sit today. It's good to mix it up every now and then. Right, Leo?"

"Yeah." Leo stared at the gooey mess on his tray.

The normally loud kid was quiet, and the quiet one was talking. What was going on? I sat and held my granola bar under my nose. "Is something wrong?"

Tyler nodded, but Leo didn't look up from his tray. Instead, he pushed mashed potatoes in circles. Tyler elbowed him.

Leo muttered, "I'm sorry for being a jerk this morning."

I dropped the granola bar. Zeke stopped, mouth open, his sandwich an inch from his mouth. Liz blinked.

Phoebe choked on the chunk of apple she'd been chewing. Leo raised his hand to pound her back, but she twisted to face him and raised her finger for him to wait. She hacked, took a drink of water, and swallowed. "You're what?"

"Sorry." His voice lowered. "I just wanted to help like I did in Cone's office."

"How did you help in Cone's office?" Phoebe said.

Leo looked at her then surveyed the rest of us. "Wasn't it obvious?" When no one nodded, he sighed. "It was clear you guys didn't know how to act in there. I've perfected the art of interaction with Mr. Cone: take responsibility to deflect anger and promise to improve to promote hope. He sees me as his *project* student."

I couldn't imagine why.

"So you think you helped us in Mr. Cone's office?" Liz pushed her glasses up as if preparing to argue.

"At least we didn't get detention." Leo shrugged and swirled the potatoes on his tray. "But I didn't want you guys to stop the Mr. P gift project. Honestly, I just wanted to help. I'm a great leader."

"Maybe..." Tyler swallowed a spoonful of pudding. "We could restart. All of us try working together again. Just do it better this time."

"Actually," Phoebe said and smirked at me. "Mouse's gift project hasn't ended. Maybe you could work with her and Zeke."

Leo's and Tyler's eyes widened. Their eyebrows arched. Both leaned against the table, waiting for a response.

No, no, no, no. "I don't know if that would work." I turned to Zeke. Chewing, he said nothing, but I could read his expression: *that would be a terrible idea.*

When I turned back to Leo and Tyler, they were staring at their trays. Shoulders sagging, Tyler said, "We get it."

Ugh. Every fiber of my body hated the idea of working with them, but I hated destroying their hope even more. "Yesterday Zeke and I learned it was hard to merge our ideas, but today we agreed on a new path. What if we write the basic story and then you guys contribute a few details to it?"

Leo and Tyler stopped playing with their food and looked up.

Around the table, surprised expressions filled my friends' faces. My new plan surprised me too.

Tyler smiled, and Leo said, "So we can help?"

"When we get to a point where we need input, yes."

"And what about the rest of us?" Crossing her

arms, Phoebe tilted her head to the side. Beside her Liz nodded in solidarity.

Next to me, Zeke had put his sandwich down and stopped eating.

Though Zeke and I had agreed to work together, I'd just made a significant decision without consulting him. And now our friends wanted to join, and I was about to make the same mistake twice. How did I get myself into these situations?

I turned to Phoebe and Liz. "Of course you can help. So can Ava." Then I turned to Zeke. "But my ideas master and I have to discuss how this is going to work and then get back to all of you. Zeke, can we talk?" I pointed to an empty table on the edge of the cafeteria.

No one had sat at that table since a kid barfed all over it a year ago. The janitors had cleaned it multiple times. The smell of bleach still surrounded it, but no one had ventured anywhere near.

Zeke stared at that table as if debating, then nodded. We gathered our items and moved.

As soon as we sat, he said, "I understand why you did it. Doesn't mean I like it."

"I'm sorry." I meant it, for multiple reasons.

He scratched his head, but didn't open his lunch

bag. "I probably would've done the same thing if I were in your place. So let's move on. How do you want to handle this?"

"Let's just write the story, then let them read it and offer ideas."

"And how do *we* write the story?" Zeke motioned between himself and me. "Agreeing on a basic story concept didn't go so smoothly for us."

He had a point. How could two people make a story together? Every word, every sentence would be debated. "I don't know."

We stared at the blank sheet of paper between us.

The clock was ticking, and we seemed farther from a gift now than when the idea first came up days ago.

Mr. P had said the hardest part of writing a story was getting the first words on the page.

I unsheathed my pencil sword and wrote on our blank sheet:

Far in the future, in a universe light years away…

Zeke smiled. "I like it. At least we have a beginning. That's something."

And that had taken me a half hour to come around on. We'd never finish this gift on time working at this pace. We needed a different plan. "I have an idea, but I don't think you're going to like it."

His eyes narrowed. "Try me."

"What if we come up with an outline for the story, something we agree on together. We can work on it today and tomorrow. Then I can use the weekend to write a first draft. On Monday, you can have first input to it, and after we make your changes, the others can see it. We'll find something of theirs to add in."

Zeke drummed his fingers against the table, staring at the sheet of paper that now had one line on it. "This gift was your idea from the beginning. It seems only right that you'd write most of it." He turned to me. "I think it's a great plan."

I released a pent up breath I hadn't known I'd been holding. "Any ideas on what our story will be about?"

"A Light Spectrum Master, his apprentice students, and an evil Dark Lord." He smiled. "And I'm guessing you had real life people in mind for each of those characters."

"Not exactly." I'd remembered Mr. P had cautioned us about using real people and real situations in our stories, but there were ways around that. "More like stereotypes that real people may or may not fit into."

"In that case, we need the characters to accomplish something significant, something like what we've learned." He snapped his fingers. "It can be symbolic."

I cracked my knuckles and prepared to plunge into a whole new universe.

Chapter 9

"Most people have finished their free writes already, and for those of you who have, today will be a sit-back-and-read day for you. For those who haven't finished, the free write will be due by the end of tomorrow." Mr. P took the liberty to relax in a chair, propping his feet up on the end of a desk.

I loved when he did that.

Ava raised her hand and blurted, "Are we allowed to write instead?"

"For sure." Mr. P smiled.

Across the table from me, Zeke pulled out our story. Though I hadn't completely finished it over the weekend, most of it was done, so I'd given it to him this morning, and he'd read over it. When I'd asked him for feedback, he'd said, "I need some soak time."

At lunch he'd read the story again and given me

the same response when I'd asked what he thought.

If he didn't like it, I wished he'd tell me so we could fix it. Soak time was over. I whipped out my pencil and pointed at the story lying on the table between us, locked in. "What do you want to change?"

Someone bumped into my back. "What's that?" Leo said over my shoulder.

I could smell his curiosity. "It's the first draft of the story." I never took my eyes off my work or Zeke. His expression was unreadable.

"Can I read it?" Leo said.

Zeke offered the pages, and Leo snatched them.

As the papers passed by, I noticed they were unmarked. Was the story so bad it wasn't worthy of fixing? If it'd been good, Zeke would have said something. He still hadn't commented.

Behind me, Leo made humming noises. "You know what this story really needs?"

The person's whose feedback I wanted, wouldn't speak, and the one I couldn't keep quiet, was happy to give input.

Leo paused as if to increase the dramatic effect. "The bad guy needs superpowers."

"Bad guy?" Tyler wandered over.

"Yeah, man. Read this story, or well, part of the first page. That's what I did." Leo handed the papers to Tyler.

My stomach seized. Zeke still hadn't commented on the story. What if there was a fatal flaw and these guys had a chance to see it before I could fix it? Zeke and Leo hadn't asked for my consent to pass it on. Now it was too late.

Tyler glanced at the papers then dropped them on the table. "Superpowers? Nah, man. This dude needs gadgets like Batman."

Leo nodded. "That would be awesome."

"A grappling hook." Tyler raised a finger like flicking on a light bulb. "No, a tractor beam!"

"And he would have cool weapons too." Leo shot imaginary guns, or maybe they were phasers.

"Indestructible vests of sheer steel!" Tyler puffed his chest out, and Leo pretended to punch it and break his hand.

Leo and Tyler posed, puny muscles flexed, and Leo said, "Everyone knows the villain is the most important part of the story."

No one believed that.

"Sounds intriguing." Zeke rubbed his chin like he had a goatee. "Maybe you could sketch a picture with all the important parts labeled. Then we could discuss what might fit the story."

"Come on, dude, let's get some paper and draw this guy out." Tyler headed to his seat, and Leo followed.

Zeke leaned across the table and pointed to his head. "Idea specialist present." He glanced at Tyler and Leo who were pulling a paper back and forth between them. "They should be busy for a while."

At least he'd done something to help. "You hate the story, don't you?"

"No." His eyebrows furrowed. "Why would you think that?"

"You've avoided giving me feedback all day."

"No, I didn't. I've been trying to figure out what to say."

"Is it that bad?" I winced and turned my head as if it would deflect the blow of his critique.

He pulled the story closer to himself and stared at it. "There's only one mention of a villain on this page." He tilted his face up then turned to Leo and Zeke, who were still fighting over the blank sheet between them. "How did that spur so much excitement?"

"You're still avoiding feedback."

"Sorry." He pushed the papers across the table to me. "The story is good, but it's missing something."

"Well, yeah, it doesn't have an ending yet."

"No, not just the ending. Something else." He stared at the paper as though in deep thought, or maybe he was stalling again.

"What does it need? Please don't say it's missing a villain with superpowers or a runaway vampire romance."

Zeke wrinkled his nose. At least we were in agreement on that.

"I don't know what it's missing. That's what I've been trying to figure out all day." He shook his head. "Maybe I'll think of it later. It looks awesome though."

How could it be awesome and still missing something? I skimmed through the characters' dialogue. Nothing stood out. Were the descriptions not thorough enough? Was the book even worth reading?

"Please get ready for afternoon announcements." The salesman voice was back, so I recited the closing script with it.

I'd have to figure this out at home.

Chapter 10

"How was school today?" Mom called from the kitchen with her typical greeting.

"Fine." My customary one-word response would satisfy her until I left the mudroom. As I slid my feet out of my shoes, a strong odor overwhelmed me. Grabbing two sneaker balls, I shoved them into the reeking spaces. Then I tossed the sneakers onto the rug like a pair of grenades and ran into the kitchen.

Mom placed a roast in the oven, and my mouth watered at the thought of eating dinner in a few hours. When she closed the oven door, her glasses were fogged. "Everything all right?"

How could she tell something was off through fog-coated lenses? "I have this one...problem."

The sound of footsteps thundered down the staircase and Brody appeared, waving a yellow piece of paper. "Look at this!"

Mom snagged the paper from his fingers as he circled the island.

"What is it?" She wiped her glasses with her shirt then returned them to her face and checked the sheet again. "A field trip."

"Not just *any* field trip. A trip to the bowling alley and laser tag!" He waved his hand in the air. "We're studying kinetic energy and Newton's Law."

"Just look in a mirror and take notes," Mom muttered. Glancing at the sheet, she put her hand on her hip. "So this is what science is coming to."

"The future is bright for all of us!" Brody circled the island then careened into the living room and bounced on the couch.

"The end-of-school-year chaos drives a lot of insanity." Sighing, Mom dropped the permission slip on the island. "Stop jumping on the furniture!"

Brody bounced off the couch and dashed upstairs.

Time to get the train back on its tracks and deal with my end-of-school-year chaos. "So, mom? I still have this problem."

"Oh, yes. Go ahead." She pulled out a kitchen chair and plopped in it, stretching her legs as though she had just finished a mile. Maybe she had.

"I'm making a story for Mr. P as a gift before he leaves."

She nodded.

"And I shared it with friends at school. They thought it was missing something, but they didn't know what. How can I fix something if I don't know what's wrong?"

Her eyebrows pinched and her lips twisted in her classic thinking cap expression. She stared at me, well, more like through me.

Like a patient being diagnosed at the doctor's office, I held onto my seat and waited.

"You know, I've always found the hardest part of writing is self-discovery." Mom's gaze landed on me. "Your classmates see something you don't. That can be hard to take."

"I can handle feedback, Mom. I just need to know what it is."

"They might not be able to express what they're seeing yet. It might take writing and rewriting, but you have to stay open to their suggestions. In time, it'll come into focus. That's how it works for me."

She wanted me to stay open to classmates who wanted to turn my book into a vampire romance that included a villain buff with weapons and superpowers. "I'm not sure that's a good idea."

Mom smiled the way she did when she thought she knew something I didn't but wanted me to discover it myself. Leaning forward, she smacked my knee. "You might be pleasantly surprised with the story it becomes if you allow others to help."

Help sounded an awful lot like complete revision, and I didn't have the time or patience for that.

Chapter 11

Ideas stopped flowing. I'd had writing slumps before, but this one had the worst timing.

In the algebra classroom, my story lay on the table, staring at me, mocking me. I was hopelessly lost.

My classmates gathered around and stared at it too. The girls and Zeke had read it, and all agreed something was missing. No one knew what. Leo and Tyler had managed to read one excerpt about the villain then agreed their ideas wouldn't work. Still, they stuck around, determined to help.

"Writing a story of this size is really complex." Ava, whose curls had lost their bounce, slumped in her seat and knocked Phoebe's binder off the table. No one reached for it.

Liz opened a bag of granola but didn't take a handful. "That's why authors get paid to write." She tossed the bag into the center of the table, offering it to the rest of the group. "It's hard to make an amazing idea come to life."

Even Leo, the king of food thievery, didn't touch the snack. He stared at Tyler's and his scribble of a villain and mumbled, "Ditto. No life here."

"Maybe our villain doesn't fit the story, but I still think the sketch looks cool." Tyler tilted his head to the side and squinted at the drawing. "You just have to stare at it for a bit."

Zeke narrowed his eyes at their paper then shook his head.

"Any new ideas for an ending, Mouse?" Phoebe tilted her head toward the papers on the table. "Maybe that's all it needs to come together."

How could an ending plug an unidentified hole? "If we knew what was missing..." But we didn't. We'd all thought about it. Well, except for Leo and Tyler who'd only mourned their villain. No one knew what the problem was. "I wanted the perfect gift for Mr. P. He deserves it."

Nodding, the others stared at the papers on the table.

Would we have to settle for merely *all right*? A pit grew in my throat. Maybe we should have gone with the cookies or card.

"This one time, I was struggling with my writing. It was due by the end of humanities class." Leo fiddled with his pencil, flipping it around his fingers then from one hand to the next. "Mr. P helped me brainstorm new ideas, and I finished before the end of class. I didn't think I could."

Leo finished an assignment on time? Mr. P was more of a miracle worker than I'd realized.

"One time, I was offered the lead role in a play." Ava wrapped one of her curls around her finger then did the same with another. "I didn't know if I wanted to take it or not. I was nervous, and well, you know how I sometimes have trouble..." Her fingers tangled in her hair. Tugging, she managed to yank free, leaving a few knots behind. "Anyway, Mr. P convinced me to take it, and it was the best experience I ever had."

Risk taker. Mr. P pushed us to take risks, smart risks. And regardless the result, he was always proud that we stepped up. Even times when I felt like I'd failed, Mr. P was there to lend perspective and let me know how proud he was that I'd taken the chance.

"One time I forgot the difference between a verb

and an adjective. Brain dead moment." Tyler smacked his head. Leo raised his hand to get in another whack, but Tyler caught his wrist. "Mr. P corrected me, and made a joke showing he was confident I knew the answer and just needed a coffee jolt that morning."

Mr. P always showed confidence in us, especially when things weren't going well and we had no confidence in ourselves.

"One time I was nervous to present in front of a class of kids older than me," Liz said. "Mr. P stayed afterschool so I could practice presenting to him and build confidence." She picked Phoebe's folder off the floor and put it by Ava as if confident she wouldn't knock it off again.

Mom always said Mr. P would go the extra mile because he cared about his students.

"I hated failing, and when I did, I was disappointed in myself," Zeke said. "Mr. P taught me that mistakes and failing are part of how we learn."

The growth mindset had to appear at some point. It was foundational to Mr. P's teaching philosophy. It was core to his being.

My story hadn't captured that. It hadn't

captured any of the ways my friends talked about him. I'd so diligently kept Mr. P the hero that I hadn't portrayed him accurately. He was a hero, but not in the conventional manner I'd written. He was more than that. My classmates were painting a better picture of him than I had.

I pulled out a new sheet of paper and scribed the stories everyone shared.

Mr. P the brainstormer and miracle worker. Mr. P the helper and risk taker. Mr. P the fervent fan and teacher. My brain whirred to life as ideas flooded my imagination.

Zeke's gaze met mine, and I mouthed three words to him: The missing piece.

Chapter 12

The Ultimate Teacher Gift
Written By: Cassie
Contributions By: Zeke, Ava, Liz, Phoebe,
Leo, and Tyler

Far in the future, in a universe light years away…

Dark Lord Bias has risen, brainwashing subjects to think only in black and white. In a remote part of the galaxy, on Planet Education, Light Spectrum Master Ja'an Ponace trains a small band of apprentices to see the color spectrum.

Lord Bias has located Master Ponace and is traveling with his troops to destroy the Light Spectrum Master and his apprentices.

Scene One: *Light Spectrum School on Planet Education*

A cough echoed through the room, interrupting scribbling pencils. Apprentice Zellius gripped his forehead in frustration. Apprentice Miz stared out the windows of the academy, toward the clear sky and purple plains, where the wind blew through fields.

Apprentices Tex and Pix wished they were out there too.

"I can't do this!" Apprentice Link flung his stylus across the table. "Master Ponace, it's too hard, and it's a perfectly good day outside." He pointed at the window and looked back at his master.

"This is of utter importance, Link." Master Ponace meditated with his eyes closed, levitating above a colorful and worn carpet. "Theorizing alternative motivations is a good exercise. It opens your mind to endless possibilities and promotes understanding."

"But it's so hard." Apprentice Link groaned and turned toward the window. Outside, a child played with a kite, running around the fields. Apprentice Link quickly looked away, afraid jealousy would consume him.

"Hard," Master Ponace said, "but not impossible." He pointed at the paper in front of Apprentice Link. "What motivations did you list for Kyel not sharing his lunch?"

"Because he's a supernova dud." Link underlined the words, four times.

"All right," Master Ponace said, "and what are other possible motivations?"

"He's a supernova dud. There is no other explanation." Apprentice Link continued to underline the words. His stylus ripped the paper.

Master Ponace sighed. "What if you were Kyel? Why would you not share your lunch? Are you a supernova dud too?"

"No." Apprentice Link dropped his stylus. "Maybe I was starving. Or maybe I promised to give it to Tex. Or maybe the guy who asked for my lunch is a supernova bully."

Master Ponace nodded. "Good. Write those on your paper."

"Why are you having us do this, Master?" Apprentice Lyra, the only student with glasses, sat in one corner of the room. "Why do you have us study this? What test are we preparing for?"

Apprentices Pix and Miz grew attentive, and Apprentice Tex sat up in his seat.

"Young Lyra, there are many challenges you can not know in advance. I have devoted today toward preparing for them."

"And yesterday..." Apprentice Link grumbled to himself.

"Master?"

The class diverted their attention to Apprentice Annora, a girl with uncontrollable curls in her hair.

"What kind of test calls for a spreadsheet?" She held up her papers in disgust and then clumsily dropped them. As her hands danced around the floor in a frenzy to pick up the papers, giggling spread around the class.

Master Ponace eyeballed each apprentice until their gazes traveled to the floor, and the laughter was vanquished. "As your teacher, I have sworn to protect the sacred ways of spectrum thinking. The spreadsheet is a tool to help." Master Ponace regarded Annora. "It was an intelligent question. Never stop asking questions."

"Who would jeopardize them? The ways of spectrum

thinking, I mean." Apprentice Lyra pushed her glasses higher on her nose.

Master Ponace raised his fingers to his temples and closed his eyes. Bright light shone around his body as he levitated, and the apprentices closed and shielded their eyes.

When they opened them, Master Ponace was standing on the old carpet, and the bright light turned into an image. A scene like one from a view screen floated around the room. Hundreds of balls of light comprised an image.

In awe, Apprentices Zellius and Pix intently examined each light fleck in the sequence. Apprentice Miz reached out to touch one, then pulled her hand back, afraid she'd break it.

"Free will cannot be controlled," the Master said. "Our individual thoughts make us unique."

The tiny balls of light shifted to form an image of a person, and a cloud floated to the top of his head. The cloud filled with color and spectacular designs. The figure put its finger to its chin, thinking.

Master Ponace continued, "But there are beings in this universe who have become so weak, living under cunning and evil forces, that they cease to carry this *ability."*

The sequence changed, and the beautiful array of lights turned dull and grayed.

"They live in a world with no color," the Master said. "Every answer, every thought, is black or white. Yes or no. Some have lost the ability to produce new ideas on their own."

Apprentices Miz and Pix gasped in horror, and Apprentice Zellius closed his eyes and tried to image such limitations.

"Yes, apprentices, it is true," Master Ponace said. "These beings are to be pitied. They've been brainwashed to believe free-thinking is an assault, that color and change are enemies of growth."

The light sequence grew darker and darker until it dissolved completely.

"Beings like Lord Bias?"

All eyes turned to Apprentice Link who sat in his chair, more attentive than ever.

Apprentice Lyra's eyebrows rose. "He's a legend, Link, a mere myth."

Across the room, Annora nervously fumbled with her pencil and dropped it on the floor. "Are you s-sure?"

"Black and white beings exist, apprentices." Master Ponace sternly peered at each of them. "Dark Lord Bias has manipulated them."

"Well, they'd be no match for my skills and power." Apprentice Link stood and placed his foot on his chair, chest puffed out, hands on his hips.

"If only I had a needle to pop that balloon you call a head." Frowning, Apprentice Lyra crossed her arms.

"Apprentices, you must understand the importance of preparation. We must be like our forefathers who trained for years to master the ways of spectrum thinking and who combated monochromatic control. Lord Bias does exist, and he presents a new threat to the galaxy. We are one of the few training grounds left. For..." Master Ponace surveyed his class.

Apprentices Link and Tex kicked dirt at each other under their desks, while Apprentice Pix yawned and Apprentice Annora twiddled her thumbs. Apprentices Lyra, Zellius, and Miz huddled together and laughed.

Master Ponace sighed. When would they learn? He could not lose another student.

Chapter 13

Scene Two: *Aboard Dark Lord Bias's Spaceship Intolerance*

Metal boots clanked along a walkway. A square cloak rode on the back of a dark figure. White robotic soldiers lined the walkway and stared blankly ahead, their arms stiffly by their sides.

The figure on the walkway snapped his fingers. "Soldier AR-5764, report."

Soldier AR-5764 stepped to the front and read off a monitor strapped to his wrist. "Yes, Lord Bias." His voice was monotone. "Multiple heat sources detected on Planet Education. A Light Spectrum Master and his apprentices. No signs of escape. No signs of awareness of us, sir."

"Perfect." Lord Bias's body was a complex mix of angular shapes. His nose was a pointed right triangle, his torso was a sharp three-dimensional rectangle, and his fingernails were squares. He looked like something out of the recycling bin, but he'd lost all color. Everything was black and white, along with his soldiers. Color was outlawed, of course.

"Those fools wouldn't notice a star if it collapsed right next to them," Bias said.

Still standing at attention, Lord Bias's minions repeated, "Fools."

"They wouldn't even see us waltz through the front door." Lord Bias stroked his pointy chin with his rectangular fingers. "This is the perfect time to attack."

The soldiers repeated, "Attack."

Lord Bias threw his head back and then spat on the floor. "Chromatic lovers. Disgusting. Just thinking about all the colors makes my eyes hurt."

The soldiers spat on the floor in unison. "Chromatic lovers. Disgusting."

"They're free-thinking, uncontrolled, open to possibilities," Lord Bias ranted. "You never know what they might suggest next. Will they take over the entire planet or make themselves a galactic smoothie? It's sheer chaos. Possibilities are the worst." Lord Bias crossed his flat-sided arms.

"Possibilities are the worst," the soldiers yelled.

"Minions," Lord Bias shouted, "stand with me as I begin my conquest to relieve this universe of spectrum thinking and instill monochromatic dominance."

"Monochromatic dominance!" On both sides of the walkway, the soldiers raised their fists in unison.

"Starting," Lord Bias shouted over the soldiers, who quieted almost automatically, "with Planet..." Lord Bias pointed at a long glass window, which gazed upon a dusty, purple planet. "Education!"

His soldiers chanted, "Attack Planet Education."

As their chorus repeated and rose, Lord Bias glared at the planet. It wouldn't be long until he eliminated the galaxy's imperfections and obtained his revenge.

Chapter 14

Scene Three: *Light Spectrum School on Planet Education*

"That's it. Keep going. Fill your mind with possibilities. Colorful, creative ideas." Master Ponace raised his eyebrows. His apprentices were close to levitating.

"I...almost...have it!" A bead of sweat collected on Apprentice Link's brow. He swiped at the sweat, lost concentration, and tumbled to the floor again. "This is stupid. Why can't you just levitate us?"

"You must master this skill yourself, Link." Master Ponace suppressed a sigh. Apprentice Link was too quick to give up. He had to embrace the spectrum for himself, or all the master's lessons would fail in the moment of true testing.

"Over here, Master Ponace!" Apprentice Pix had

gotten higher than the others, but she lost focus when Apprentice Annora bumped into her. Both fell to the ground. Glaring, Apprentice Pix snapped, "Annora, control your body!"

"Sorry." Apprentice Annora's shoulders drooped. "It was an accident."

Master Ponace extended his hand to her. "Mistakes are the stepping stones to success." He helped Annora to her feet. "Never give up. Every time you try, you grow."

She nodded, and he turned to Apprentice Pix. "To master spectrum thinking, one must be aware of those around them—their thoughts, their feelings, their history. This promotes understanding, which is a great power."

"How is understanding a power?" Tex hopped from one foot to the other, attempting to levitate via jumping and hang time. "Did you already teach us this, and I wasn't listen...?" He stopped, and his face reddened. "I mean, um, I forgot?"

Master Ponace suppressed another sigh. "Understanding opens our minds to possibilities, where we find alternate solutions, explanations, and answers. Understanding allows us to accept others, even if we disagree with them. Understanding promotes compassion and kindness, which are priceless traits. Understanding —"

"Is a good thing." Apprentice Link picked himself off the floor again. "We get it."

But did they really? Master Ponace wasn't sure. Only a real test would reveal the truth.

"Master Ponace?" Apprentice Miz levitated a few inches from the floor. Beside her, Apprentices Zellius and Lyra were hovering over the ground as well. The space between them and the floor was small but growing.

The master put both thumbs up and grinned. "Excellent, apprentices." He pointed to them and turned to the others. "All of you can do this. You have brainstormed possibilities and recorded them on your sheets. Now remember the Kyel lunch case study, remember the many motivations, and open your minds to more possibilities."

Apprentices Pix and Annora closed their eyes and began to levitate.

The master's heart raced like a spaceship at warp speed. He added, "Develop solutions to the case study. Imagine how you could respond and react to Kyel when he refuses to share his lunch. What would promote understanding, peace, and growth?"

The students rose higher in the air, and even Apprentices Link and Tex began to levitate.

"Master Ponace, look!" Apprentice Lyra's eyes were

wide, and she lowered until her sandals touched the floor.

"What's wrong?" Master Ponace watched the other students drop to the ground beside her.

Apprentice Annora gaped, while Apprentices Pix and Miz stepped back.

Apprentice Zellius pointed. "Someone's on the other side of the door."

Master Ponace's eyebrows furrowed with suspicion, and he spun around.

The doors flung open and crashed into the walls behind them.

Dark Lord Bias stepped into the classroom. He wore a malevolent smile as his soldiers fanned out, blasters by their sides, behind him. They stomped in rhythm, as if they were marching to the beat of a drum.

The apprentices' eyes widened in fear as the soldiers looped around the room and corralled the class and Master Ponace.

"Ponace, I'm surprised that as disgustingly colorful as your thinking is, you've forgotten to turn on your defense system." Lord Bias scoffed and studied the classroom. His beady, rhombus-shaped eyes scanned the apprentices. "Truly untrustworthy."

Around the room, his soldiers chuckled and repeated, "Untrustworthy."

Apprentices Lyra, Pix, and Annora gulped, while Apprentices Zellius and Miz held their breath. They felt small, and their confidence drained.

Apprentices Link and Tex exchanged a glance. Then trembling, Link called out, "We aren't afraid of you."

Lord Bias smiled wickedly at Apprentice Link, who hid behind Apprentice Tex.

"Spectrum thinking. What a joke." Lord Bias laughed, and so did his minions. "Never any solid ground. Maybe this. Maybe that. Wouldn't it be easier to have one right answer? One proper way? One universal opinion? Your master is making your lives hard for no reason. Ponace is untrustworthy."

His soldiers repeated, "Untrustworthy."

Master Ponace frowned and stared at Lord Bias with a hard, unwavering gaze.

The apprentices looked up to examine their master's expression. A tight knot of doubt began to bunch up in their chests.

"Now, monochromatic thinking..." Lord Bias threw his head back and raised his pointy nose to the ceiling, taking in a deep breath of air as if it revived him. "Oh, how it soothes the soul. No need to tire oneself coming up with possibilities. One thought. One answer. One way. Simple black and white." Lord Bias raised an eyebrow toward the apprentices. "Pure black and white. I can show you the way."

Master Ponace bent down on a knee to address his paling apprentices. "He's trying to poison your minds. Fight it. Resist it."

"Bah, he's lying," said Lord Bias. "I am the Dark Lord, I know all! How can you trust a teacher who makes your life unnecessarily hard and doesn't even turn the security system on to protect you? Join my monochromatic ranks and live an easy, protected life."

His soldiers said, "Lord Bias knows all," and then they sang, "Monochromatic purity."

To Master Ponace's dismay, the color drained from his students' faces. Blonde, red, and brown hair faded. Their eyes weren't as blue, brown, or green.

Apprentice Link tapped Apprentice Tex on the shoulder. "Could Lord Bias be right?"

"Monochromatic...purity?" murmured Apprentices Pix and Annora.

"Students, remember what I taught you," Master Ponace called. "Find alternate explanations, never stop asking questions, imagine!"

Lord Bias sneered. "Apprentices, your master isn't trustworthy. He's failed you."

"What if," Apprentice Miz quietly said, "there was a

different reason why the defense system wasn't working?"

"Brilliant," Master Ponace said.

"Preposterous," Lord Bias exclaimed. "Ponace forgot to turn on the security system. That's the only reason."

"Untrustworthy," his soldiers chanted.

"What if..." Apprentice Lyra struggled to come up with a simple idea. "What if the battery died?"

Apprentice Zellius cried, "What if Lord Bias hacked it?"

"Yes, yes," Master Ponace urged them.

"No," Lord Bias screeched. "Ponace failed. You can't trust him."

"Untrustworthy." The minions carried the refrain.

Apprentice Annora stumbled forward. "What if there was a malfunction?"

"What if Annora ran into it again?" Apprentice Pix blurted.

"What if I did it?" Apprentice Link stepped from behind Apprentice Tex. The other apprentices glared at him, and Apprentice Link added, "Just throwing out possibilities, not facts."

"What if the window was open during a rainy day, and the water fizzled the system?" Apprentice Tex shouted.

The apprentices' hair and eyes blazed with color. They had returned to their normal, vibrant state.

Master Ponace clapped excitedly. "Exceptional. Quite exceptional."

"Agh." Lord Bias clenched his teeth and spat. The apprentices had almost turned. They just needed another push. "Someone is always at fault, even if there was an accident, even if there was a malfunction. Someone wasn't careful. Someone didn't do a maintenance check." He pointed at Apprentice Link. "Was it you?"

"Me?" The apprentice pointed at himself. He glanced at Apprentice Tex then his classmates and shook his head. "I didn't do it."

"You then?" Lord Bias pointed at Apprentice Annora, and she fell over.

"It wasn't me."

"Someone is to blame." Lord Bias glared at each of the students. "And I'll find out who."

"Apprentices." Master Ponace laced his fingers and lowered his hands in front of himself as if a prisoner. "It was I who shut off the defense system."

Speechless, the apprentices gaped.

Lord Bias grinned at Master Ponace. "Traitor!" He surveyed the apprentices. "Ponace never cared for your well-being. He threw you under the intergalactic bus."

"Traitor," the soldiers chanted.

"You shut off the defense system, Master Ponace?" Apprentice Lyra stepped toward her teacher, and when he didn't respond, she turned to Apprentice Zellius. "Could it be true?"

Their colors began to drain again.

"We could die," Apprentice Pix said to Apprentice Miz, and their colors faded too.

Master Ponace said nothing. If his students were to embrace spectrum thinking, they'd need to practice his lessons now. If they didn't...

No, these students were stronger than the student he'd lost. They would pass the test. He believed in them, whether or not they believed in him right now.

"Your master has proven untrustworthy. He's failed you." Lord Bias extended his hands and stepped deeper into the classroom. The apprentices were losing color rapidly. It wouldn't be long before they were black and white, before they were his. "Monochromatic ways are simple to follow. They bring order. They create uniformity."

Only the faintest hue remained on the apprentices' blanched skin. Eyes wide with fear, they glanced at their master then studied each other. As a group, they slowly turned to Lord Bias.

He grinned, confident his plan had worked.

Somber, Master Ponace closed his eyes as if praying. Colors radiated from him, casting an aura.

Lord Bias chuckled. "Your colors won't help you n—"

"No!" Apprentice Annora cried aloud. She stepped between her classmates and Lord Bias and faced her friends. "Don't you realize? This is what Master Ponace wanted. He wanted to prepare us," she said and gestured toward Lord Bias, "for the test unknown."

"He's testing us?" Apprentice Link's mouth gaped, utterly stunned.

"Teaching us," Apprentice Lyra exclaimed. "Like that one time when we had to present in front of others. He was teaching us self-confidence, even if we didn't realize it."

"Yeah! During the levitating session, he was teaching us to brainstorm," Apprentice Zellius shouted from the back of the crowd.

"All along, Master Ponace was mentoring and preparing us for our future..." Apprentice Miz turned around to face Master Ponace, who beamed at his class.

"And we didn't believe him," Apprentice Pix said.

"Until now," Apprentice Tex finished.

The students' color revived. Auras surrounded each one like a shield.

"Well done, apprentices." Master Ponace gave his students thumbs up. His pride swelled like a balloon.

"No." Lord Bias gasped in horror. How had this happened?

Master Ponace slowly turned, making eye contact with all of Lord Bias's army. "There is a reason I left the shields down." He paced between soldiers and apprentices. "Many years ago, Lord Bias was my student, but he couldn't see color in my teachings. He chose to see only black and white."

A collective gasp escaped from the apprentices. The soldiers' heads swiveled left and right, looking at each other, wondering if the others had heard the same thing.

The master continued, "I turned off the defense system, not only to teach you..." He waved his arm toward the apprentices, then turned to Lord Bias. "But also to give my former student a second chance." Master Ponace extended his hand to Lord Bias, who stared at it.

After all these years, the master still held out hope. Why? Lord Bias could never accept color, not before, not now.

The master's outstretched hand beckoned. "Black and white are colors we paint with. They have a place." He smiled at his former student. "But learn to see the other colors. See the possibilities. Understand others instead of trying to control them. It's about unity, not uniformity. I can teach you."

Lord Bias still stared at the outstretched hand. The master had taught these students to embrace color. Each of them was unique, but they held to the same vision. They'd clung to spectrum thinking even in the face of his monochromatic force.

"Bob," Master Ponace said, "I still believe in you."

He did? Lord Bias raised his hand. Twinkles of hues formed at his fingertips. Was it possible that spectrum thinking was better than monochromatic? Slowly color spread along his fingers. His sharp edges began to curve, pigment flushed into his fingernails.

But how could he live without rules? There would be no order, no limits, no control. That wasn't a world he wanted to live in. "No... never..." Lord Bias stumbled back and glared at Master Ponace.

The master stepped toward him. "Bob, you have options. This doesn't have to end just one of two ways. Compromise. Take it slow. Try spectrum thinking before making a full commitment one way or another."

"No." Lord Bias covered his ears and stepped back again.

"Please, Bob." Master Ponace remained in place but stretched out his hand farther.

Lord Bias backpedaled to the door. "Minions, follow me."

The soldiers didn't move. Slowly, one lowered his blaster to the floor then raised his arms and placed his armored hands on his helmet. He removed his helmet, revealing a boy with curly hair like Apprentice Annora. He surveyed the other soldiers, and then his gaze landed on Master Ponace. "May I stay and learn the ways of spectrum thinking?"

"Of course." The master nodded and opened his arms wide. "Anyone is welcome."

Around the room, soldiers put their blasters on the floor and removed their helmets. A girl with frizzy orange hair appeared, so did a boy with uncontrollable freckles.

Lord Bias spat on the ground. "This isn't over. I'll never change, not even if the entire cosmos depended on it. And I'll find others who agree with me." He turned, and his cape billowed behind him and swept dust off the ground in his wake. The dust hit the front row of apprentices who shielded their eyes. When they put their arms down, Lord Bias had disappeared.

The soldiers blinked at one another, their expressions blank. Some scratched their heads, unsure of what to do. Some were simply unable to think.

Master Ponace turned to his apprentices. "You have

learned well, and I'm very proud of each of you."

Throughout the room, the apprentices stood taller.

"You have embraced spectrum thinking, and now, before me, stand not students, but masters at work. You have tapped into your limitless creativity, which so few are capable of doing. Be proud, apprentices, this is a monumental point in your training."

Apprentices Tex and Pix high-fived. Apprentice Zellius blushed, and Apprentice Link sat with his legs crossed, inches above the floor. Apprentices around the room whooped and cheered.

"But..." He paused until his apprentices stared at him. "I'm sorry to say that this inspirational moment may be our last together."

Apprentices Pix and Annora gasped.

"No." Apprentice Lyra cried.

Apprentice Link plopped on the ground.

Master Ponace's face was solemn. "It's true. I must leave. I've received an urgent request from another planet who needs a Spectrum Master."

Climbing to his feet, Apprentice Link forced a smile and shrugged. "Less work for us." Apprentice Tex elbowed Link's side, and Apprentice Link said, "I'm joking... obviously." He blushed.

"But what about Planet Education? What about us?"

Eyes pleading, Apprentice Lyra tugged on the hem of her tunic.

Master Ponace's face melted into a warm smile. "Unlike here, the other planet is desperate for spectrum thinking. I must train students there as I have trained you."

"But then who will be our master?" Apprentice Tex lifted his finger, as if pointing out a technicality.

Master Ponace spread his arms to the class of apprentices. "You have become Light Spectrum Masters. Facing Lord Bias was a test, a challenge. You have overcome." Master Ponace directed their attention to Apprentice Miz who'd closed her eyes and floated almost a foot above the ground. "You have proven yourselves and have completed your training."

Apprentice Link squeezed his eyes shut and pinched his face together. Then, he opened his eyes. "Becoming a Light Spectrum Master doesn't feel any different!"

Master Ponace chuckled and bent down on a knee to talk to his apprentices. "Do you see those soldiers over there?" He pointed to boys and girls still dressed in black and white uniforms, examining their fingers and toes as if they just discovered them. "You are to train them as I have trained you. Be patient, and be kind. Be encouraging, but be stern when you must. Let them wander and explore, as I have let you. Turn their weaknesses into strengths, and when you have done that, they will become fluent with spectrum thinking. Once they do, send them out into the galaxy."

The apprentices nodded. A look of determination and sincerity floated on Apprentice Link's brow. A flutter of worry flew into Apprentice Miz's stomach. Apprentices Tex and Lyra wore pride through a smile. They had a real mission!

"I plan to leave tomorrow morning," Master Ponace said. "But I will say goodbye to each of you before I depart."

The apprentices shared a thought: Master Ponace needed a goodbye gift so he wouldn't forget a single one of them.

***

The next day came early. Almost too early.

Master Ponace strolled through the school halls, sighing at memories as he went along.

A piece of paper crackled under Master Ponace's sandal. He bent down to examine it and saw Link's messy signature at the top of the page. Master Ponace remembered Link crumpling his paper and tossing it across the room in despair. Link believed he would never be able to finish the assignment. Master Ponace gently tossed the paper into an incinerator. Link had overcome his lack of persistence when he had battled against Lord Bias.

Master Ponace continued into the small dining court. Stone tables were set up around the room, and larger-than-life fireflies flew around, lighting the area. A broken food replicator in the corner of the room reminded him of Apprentice Annora stumbling into the small cafeteria on the first day, unsure if she could learn anything. How much she had grown.

Turning back to the hallway, a mouse scampered across the floor then paused to tilt its head up to Master Ponace. The mouse reminded Master Ponace of Apprentice Miz, the quietest of them all. She had refused to speak in front of the class. Shyness was an aura that surrounded her. Yet, Master Ponace remembered the day she had spoken up at last, and began to answer questions in class.

Memories flooded in like stars during warp drive. Master Ponace marveled at how much his apprentices had grown over the years he taught them. The bittersweet moment tugged at his heart. How much he would miss his students—but the confidence he had in their success *drove him onward.*

He strolled to his destination, the classroom where he'd taught his dear apprentices for two years.

Waiting for him, his apprentices sat in a half circle around his colorful carpet.

"What's this?" Master Ponace placed his hands on his hips.

"We wanted to give you a gift. A token of our appreciation," Apprentice Link said.

The class smiled at their master.

Apprentice Lyra came forward holding a delicate ball in her hands. It resembled a bubble with vibrant color highlights.

"It's a memory keepsake." She handed it to her teacher. "When you hold the sphere, it collects memories you have of us. Then it'll save them and replay them for you whenever you want. Look."

The bubble's insides grew foggy then showed a mini version of Apprentice Lyra, with the class sitting behind her, holding out the ball for Master Ponace to take.

"You're remembering this moment." Apprentice Lyra realized.

"I wouldn't want to forget it." Master Ponace smiled at each of his students.

"I wanted to give it to you but they wouldn't let me."

Apprentice Annora gestured to her fellow apprentices.

"It was for the best," Apprentice Tex said.

Apprentice Pix said, "We wanted you to have a functioning gift."

"Yeah, not puzzle pieces to assemble," Apprentice Lyra added.

Loud murmurs of agreement lifted in the class. Apprentice Annora blushed and then smiled.

Master Ponace glanced from his gift to his students. He would remember this moment for infinity. "Thank you for the memory keepsake gift, but the best gift is that you've embraced my teaching so now you're able to teach others."

"But what about Lord Bias?" Apprentice Link frowned and tilted his head.

"I certainly hold out hope for him, and the rest of you should too. Maybe one of you will have an opportunity to teach him in the future."

Some apprentices glanced anxiously at one another, others sat up straighter and looked hopeful.

"Now, our journeys must part. It's been an honor and a privilege to be your master. I will remember all of you, and especially this moment, thanks to the memory keepsake." Master Ponace held up the ball in one hand to show the class. The ball slipped from his fingers and fell *in slow motion.*

The apprentices bit their lips—some even turned away for a split second.

Apprentice Annora dove from the front row and grasped the ball just before it shattered on the floor. "Gotcha!" She held it out in front of her and glanced at her class, who sat with their eyes wide and jaws hanging. Annora shrugged and handed it with ease to her Master.

Apprentice Link slapped his face with both of his hands. "Did she just…?"

"Catch and save a priceless item instead of break it?" Apprentice Lyra sat stunned next to him.

Apprentice Zellius who sat in the middle row pumped his fist in the air. "Whoo! Go, Annora!"

The class laughed and joined the cheer.

"Thank you, Annora, for the amazing save." The master waited for the class cheer to quiet and added, "Never quit the amazing growth you have all shown me." Master Ponace winked at Apprentice Annora.

Apprentice Tex whispered to Apprentice Zellius, "Of course. Growth."

Master Ponace approached each of them for a final hug, a heart-warming experience.

Once they all said their goodbyes and bid their farewells, Master Ponace opened the double doors at the entrance of the training center. He faced his students as wind whipped around him and made the ends of his cloak whip in a frenzy. "You will all be my students forever."

Lights and radiant colors grew around the edges of his clothes. Vibrant colors swirled and weaved around Master Ponace's face, hands, neck, and sandals, until the apprentices could no longer see their master. Slowly, the colors diminished, and along with them, Master Ponace disappeared.

The apprentices felt a loneliness they'd never experienced before seep into their consciousness. That is until Apprentice Link spoke up. "That's the way to make an exit."

THE END

Chapter 15

I sheathed my pencil sword and smiled at the papers in front of me. The story had finally come together. Even before the others had a chance to read it, I knew it was good.

The heart of the story wasn't that Mr. P fought the villain himself, but that he'd taught his students to. *He was a hero who created heroes.*

Around the table, the rest of my friends stopped eating their lunches. After swallowing a mouth full of salad, Ava said, "Well?"

"Finished." I grabbed the papers and tapped them against the desk bringing them into alignment. Then I handed the stack to Zeke.

"Hey." Leo reached for the papers. "Why does he get to read it first? This was a team effort."

Liz blocked Leo's attempted grab. She cleared her throat, and he sat back in his seat next to Tyler.

Liz tilted her head toward me. "Technically, Mouse did all the writing, but I'd like to hear it too."

Phoebe pointed at me. "Why don't you read it to us, Mouse?"

"No." Gathering my lunch bag and binder, I stood. "Zeke can read it to you, and then you can let me know what you think. I need time away from the story."

"Burnout." Tyler snapped his fingers and picked up a chicken sandwich from his tray. "Happens to me all the time." He took a bite.

I waved goodbye to the crew, confident they'd like the ending, and headed to the cafeteria exit, which Mrs. Garcia was guarding. "I'd like to go to Mr. P's classroom. He gave me permission to hang out there whenever I need a break from the cafeteria."

"I know." She winked then tilted her head toward my friends, who huddled around the table, leaning forward to hear every word Zeke read. "Are you escaping the others?"

"No, they're helping me."

"I suppose this means you completed the special project." She smiled and added, "Without any additional *accidents*."

I nodded.

"Good." Her gaze roamed the cafeteria as if searching for trouble. She lowered her voice. "I didn't tell Mr. P, or any of the other teachers, about it."

"Thank you."

"You're welcome." She stopped scanning the cafeteria and focused on me. "The challenges you overcame to create this gift would make a great story in itself. I've been watching your group for a while, and I'm sure that he'd love to hear *that* story too."

Another lightning bolt idea hit me: why not include the story behind the story?

"Thanks, Mrs. Garcia." I rushed to the nearest open table and unsheathed my pencil sword again. Then I scrounged in my binder for a blank piece of paper.

The school year was about to end, so I'd need even more help to finish on time, but I had a good team here and at home. Working on this gift had grown my confidence, so I was convinced expanding the story would work out. And when it did, Mr. P would finally receive the ultimate teacher gift. Well, at least that's what it was in my opinion.

Cailey Appenzeller

Putting pencil to paper, I began to write:

I'm leaving

I held a sheet of paper filled with words from my teacher, but those were the only two I saw. They weren't a surprise, but they were a shock, like when you stick your finger in an electric socket. Not that I'd tried it...

About the Book

I hope you enjoyed *The Ultimate Teacher Gift*. It's a story I wrote as a farewell gift for a special middle school teacher I had.

My teacher inspired me to grow like the main character in the story. I wasn't interested in open-ended assignments or speaking in front of the class (or in front of anyone), but he challenged me to try, and then he cheered me on. He believed in me and my potential, and that made me believe in myself.

What amazed me most was he did that not just for me, but for my classmates as well. He had a unique ability to make everyone feel like he or she was his favorite.

I wrote this story both as a thank you to him, and hopefully as an inspiration for students, teachers, and parents everywhere.

If we challenge, encourage, and believe in the

people around us, that will make a difference to them—and maybe that's the greatest difference we can make.

~ Cailey